MUMMY MATH

An Adventure in Geometry

Cindy Neuschwander
illustrated by Bryan Langdo

SQUARE
FISH

Henry Holt and Company

Special thanks to my editor, Reka Simonsen,
for her vision and direction

For Bruce, Seth, and Tim with love —C. N.

For Nikki, for making me very happy —B. L.

SQUARE
FISH

An Imprint of Macmillan

MUMMY MATH. Text copyright © 2005 by Cindy Neuschwander. Illustrations copyright © 2005 by Bryan Langdo.
All rights reserved. Printed in June 2010 in China by South China Printing Co. Ltd., Dongguan City, Guangdong Province.
For information, address Square Fish, 175 Fifth Avenue, New York, N.Y. 10010.

Square Fish and the Square Fish logo are trademarks of Macmillan and are used by Henry Holt and Company under license from Macmillan.

Library of Congress Cataloging-in-Publication Data
Neuschwander, Cindy.
Mummy math: an adventure in geometry / Cindy Neuschwander; illustrated by Bryan Langdo.
p. cm.
ISBN: 978-0-312-56117-8
1. Pyramid (Geometry)—Juvenile literature. 2. Pyramids—Juvenile literature.
3. Geometry, Solid—Juvenile literature. I. Langdo, Bryan, ill. II. Title.
QA491.N48 2005
516—dc22
2004009200

Originally published in the United States by Henry Holt and Company
Square Fish logo designed by Filomena Tuosto
First Square Fish Edition: August 2009
10 9 8 7 6 5 4 3 2
www.squarefishbooks.com

The artist used Winsor & Newton watercolors on Fabriano Uno paper to create the illustrations for this book.

"Woo hoo!" cheered Matt Zills. "We're going to Egypt! I want to explore pyramids and see mummies!"

"I'm going to learn how to read hieroglyphics so I can unlock the mysteries of the tomb!" said his twin sister, Bibi.

Matt and Bibi's parents were famous scientists. Their family had been invited to Egypt to help find the mummy of an ancient pharaoh.

Dr. Zagazig, the archaeologist, greeted them when they arrived at the site. The pyramid was magnificent.

"This tomb is a complete mystery," said Dr. Zagazig. "We can't find the burial chamber anywhere."

"So the secrets of the pharaoh still await us!" said Dr. Zills eagerly. "Let's go!"

Matt, Bibi, and their dog, Riley, crawled through the tiny opening first. FWUMP! A secret door suddenly closed behind them.

"HELP!" yelled Matt. "We're locked in and they're locked out!"

"What should we do?" wondered Bibi.

"Let's go find the mummy. What else can we do?" said Matt bravely.

The walls of the tomb were covered with colorful hieroglyphics.

"What do they say?" asked Matt.

Bibi read slowly. "This king was called the Pharaoh with Many Faces. He built the most complicated Egyptian pyramid ever."

"Wow!" said Matt. "Where's a tour guide when you need one?"

"Look at all these geometric solids," said Bibi, ignoring Matt's joke. "Cones, spheres, cubes, cylinders, pyramids, tetrahedrons, and rectangular and triangular prisms."

"I wonder what they mean," said Matt.

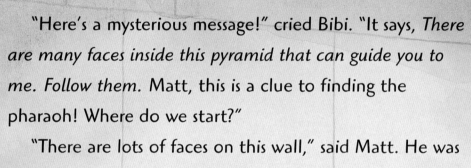

"Here's a mysterious message!" cried Bibi. "It says, *There are many faces inside this pyramid that can guide you to me. Follow them.* Matt, this is a clue to finding the pharaoh! Where do we start?"

"There are lots of faces on this wall," said Matt. He was looking at a painting of some ancient Egyptians. "They're all pointing left. Let's go that way!"

At that moment, Riley snuffled loudly and ran off into the darkness.

"He's just chasing cat mummies," joked Bibi. "He'll come back."

Matt and Bibi turned left. Suddenly the ground opened under them.

WHOOSH! They slid down a narrow shaft and landed in a small, empty room.

"Ouch!" said Matt, brushing himself off.

"This place gives me the creeps!" added Bibi.

"This'll cheer you up," said Matt. "What's a mummy's favorite music?"

"I give up," said his sister.

"Wrap music!"

"Matt, your corny jokes aren't helping us to find the pharaoh—or the way out!"

"Face it, Bibi," said Matt. "We're totally lost."

"Face it? That's it!" Bibi said excitedly. "That's what the pharaoh meant!"

Matt was confused.

"If you think about faces, what do you think of?" asked Bibi.

"People," said Matt. "And maybe mummies too."

"What else has a face? Remember that first picture?" cried Bibi. "The flat sides of a geometric solid are called faces. A cylinder has two round faces, a tetrahedron has four triangular faces, a cube has six square faces. . . ."

"So the pharaoh's clues are the faces of *solid shapes*," said Matt, "not *people's* faces!"

The twins walked up a steep corridor.

"Here's another clue!" said Bibi. "*A single face shows the way.*"

This painting showed a mason cutting a large block of limestone.

"But that block is a rectangular prism," said Bibi. "It has six faces. That's five faces too many."

"The guy shaping the stone looks like he's holding an ice cream cone." Matt giggled.

"That's the mallet they used to chip away the rock," explained Bibi. "But the top part is cone-shaped. A cone has a single face! Let's follow it."

The cone's face was pointing up, so Matt and Bibi scaled the high wall. On a ledge at the top sat a single round stone.

"That looks like an ancient Egyptian base-ball," said Matt.

"Workers used rocks like this to hammer out tunnels in the pyramids," said Bibi. "It's a sphere. But a sphere doesn't have any faces we can follow."

"Still, the only way to go is through this tunnel," said Matt, pointing to an opening in the rock.

They squeezed through the narrow space and inched along until they reached a wider area. They were dazzled by what they saw.

"Wow! Is this the burial chamber?" asked Matt.

"No," said Bibi. "I think this is the antechamber. It's the room that leads to the burial chamber. It holds everything the pharaoh might need in his next life."

"There are lots of things here I wouldn't mind having in my present life," said Matt. "Except for this 4,000-year-old bread!"

They found the next clue on
a piece of papyrus. *Look for six
identical faces*, it said.
"A cube?" guessed Matt.

"Maybe this is it," said Bibi. She held her breath and lifted the lid of a carved wooden box.

Matt laughed. "It's clean underwear for the pharaoh!"

"I guess he'd need that in his next life." Bibi giggled.

A second cube-shaped box held the clue they were searching for. It led Matt and Bibi into a room with three gigantic granite towers.

The first one was a cylinder with a cone perched on top. The second tower was a five-faced triangular prism with a tetrahedron on it. The third one was a pyramid on top of a rectangular prism. At the foot of each tower was a closed door.

"Is the pharaoh behind door number one, door number two, or door number three?" asked Matt, bowing and waving at each one.

"Get serious," said Bibi. "The clue in the box told us to enter under the five faces." There had also been a warning: *Choose carefully lest you lose your way forever.*

"I choose door number three!" said Matt. "That pyramid has four triangular faces and a square base. That makes five faces in all." He started to open the door.

"WAIT!" yelled Bibi.

She yanked her brother back. "The pyramid does have five faces, but it's resting on the top face of the rectangular prism. That makes six faces we would walk under.

I think number two is the right door. The tetrahedron has four faces, and it's sitting on one face of the triangular prism. That makes five. Let's go!"

Suddenly they heard a muffled, mysterious, shuffling sound.

"What's that?" whispered Bibi.

Matt shivered. "A real live mummy?"

They hurried through the second door. The burial chamber at last! Two rectangular coffins sat on the floor.

The shuffling sound was growing louder. Something had followed them!

"Let's find this pharaoh and get out of here!" said Matt nervously.

Bibi and Matt tiptoed toward the two dimly lit shapes. The shuffling sound began snuffling . . . and then . . . howling!

"AHH!" screamed the twins, diving behind the
nearest coffin. Bibi peeked around the side.

"Riley!" she cried. "You big, furry goofball. You scared us!"
Riley was standing by the other coffin.

Matt opened the lid and looked inside. "He found his cats!" he exclaimed.

Bibi looked too. "I'll bet these mummies were the pharoah's favorite pets!"

Then they opened the first coffin. The pharaoh's golden burial mask twinkled up at them.

"This is the last of the pharaoh's many faces," said Matt.

"But not the last of his help," Bibi pointed out. "There's a map on the coffin lid to show us the way out of this five-faced mountain of stone."

Matt grinned. "Awesome! Let's go and report back to Dad and 'Mummy'!"

A NOTE TO TEACHERS AND PARENTS

Mummy Math introduces eight common geometric solids: cone, cylinder, cube, sphere, pyramid, tetrahedron, rectangular prism, and triangular prism. The story uses these solids as clues for finding an ancient mummy. After reading this book, you can try these suggestions for fun ways to teach about geometric solids:

- Help children identify and name the solids they read about in the story. Collecting and sorting real solids is one good way to do this. Soup cans, ice cream cones, and various boxes make a good start.

- With actual solid shapes, children can build models. Re-creating the three towers in the story gives them practice in visualizing faces of shapes they can't actually see when the structures are completed. Castles, houses, space stations, and other imaginative structures can also be made.

- Have children look at diagrams of flattened geometric solids (called geometric nets) and predict which drawings represent which solids. They can then cut out these nets and fold them into their solid shapes. This activity helps them practice their spatial reasoning skills.

- Try classifying solids by the number of faces on each shape. Along with faces, children can figure out the number of edges these shapes have, as well as their vertices (or corner points). These results can be recorded on a sheet of paper or a chart. This helps children to see the attributes of each shape.

- Three-dimensional geometry is full of interesting relationships. For example, a tetrahedron is really a kind of pyramid. Children can investigate how shapes in the story are related to each other. Looking at a list of attributes may give them some good clues.

Whatever activities you try, they can help kids enjoy the math!